Kanga Klaus
Text copyright © 2010 Susan Harman & Eric Harman
Illustrations copyright © 2010 Ray Geier

Requests for permission to copy any part of this work should be mailed to:
Harman & Associates, Inc.
4302 Peach Way
Boulder, CO 80301
www.kangaklaus.com

Library of Congress Control Number: 2010932832
Kanga Klaus/ Susan Harman, Eric Harman
Boulder, CO: Harman & Associates, 2010
p. cm.
ISBN 978-0-615-38852-6 (hardcover)

First Edition

Printed in Korea

# Kanga Klaus

Eric Harman

Susan A. Harman

RAY GEIER

Ray, Susan, and Eric at the Denver Zoo

# Meet the Authors & Illustrator

**Susan Harman**, *Author*   (Center)

Susan Harman grew up in the Midwest and attended the University of Wisconsin. Travels brought her to Boulder, Colorado where she taught fifth and sixth grade for twenty years. Mrs. Harman's love for creative writing became a big part of her teaching. Each year she would help her students publish their best works. As a child, Mrs. Harman lived on a farm and developed a love for animals. Rare trips to the zoo sparked the question: "Did the zoo animals receive presents for Christmas?" The love for animals and Christmas bubbled around in Susan's head for years and became the inspiration for "Kanga Klaus."

**Eric Harman**, *Author*   (Right)

Susan's son, Eric grew up in Boulder, Colorado and graduated in Bio-Chemical Engineering. He has worked as an engineer in fluid dynamics for 30 years. Eric wrote poetry in high school and college and rediscovered his love for writing in 2007 when he collaborated with his mother in writing Kanga Klaus. Mr. Harman is happily married with two sons, a dog and two turtles named, Betty and Little "E".

**Ray Geier**, *Illustrator*   (Left)

Ray Geier grew up in the Midwest, and moved to Colorado in the mid 80's. Ray caught the artist bug about the age of five when he wowed friends drawing a decent likeness of Batman. Mr. Geier has been painting ever since and creates his art by hand using pencil, pastel, watercolor, gouache, acrylic and oil. In between projects, Ray teaches art lessons and hosts workshops. You can see Ray's work in galleries, businesses and shows throughout Colorado, and at www.raygeier.com.

# The Birth of Kanga Klaus

The idea for Kanga Klaus lay dormant in Susan's head for nearly 50 years.
In 2007, Susan and Eric began collaborating on Kanga Klaus. This mother-son
team met Saturday mornings over coffee for nine months until Kanga Klaus
was complete. During that time they wrote several other short stories.
Illustrator, Ray Geier, joined the Harman duo in February, 2010. The Boulder
trio worked daily until publication in July, 2010. Susan, Eric, and Ray live
less than a mile from each other and have become good friends.

They will be releasing several other children's book in 2011.
Check out www.KangaKlaus.com for scheduled book release dates.

# Kanga Klaus

Written by Susan & Eric Harman       Illustrated by Ray Geier

*Dedicated to all the animals on the planet, and especially to those who share their lives in the zoos and sanctuaries providing joy, happiness and educational insight for future generations.*

Christmas was coming to the great Big City Zoo.
Santa's helper was Herman the Red Kangaroo.

Next to the zoo, an old orphanage did reside,
A wrought iron fence kept children on the other side.

On Christmas Day Herman would be named Kanga Klaus,

Only if he could follow Santa's rules and laws.

The Christmas Spirit he must capture and possess.

Then with Santa, Herman would be a big success.

Requirements
to become
K. Klaus:
* Help Others
* Eat Vegetables
* Fix Sleigh
* Calm Reindeer
* Let Elves Ride
In Pouch
* Spread Christmas
Spirit often . . .

The animals prepared the zoo for Christmas Day.
Their decorations were a magical display.

Feathered, white owls hung ornaments on needle-thin trees.
Spiders spun silver webs, with the greatest of ease.

Bushy-tailed squirrels gathered chestnuts and berries.
Slippery seals sang Christmas carols so merry.

High above, white crowned eagles circled in free flight,
While below, peacocks paraded plumage so bright.

Even the old orphanage from across the way,
Took delight in the creatures' colorful display.

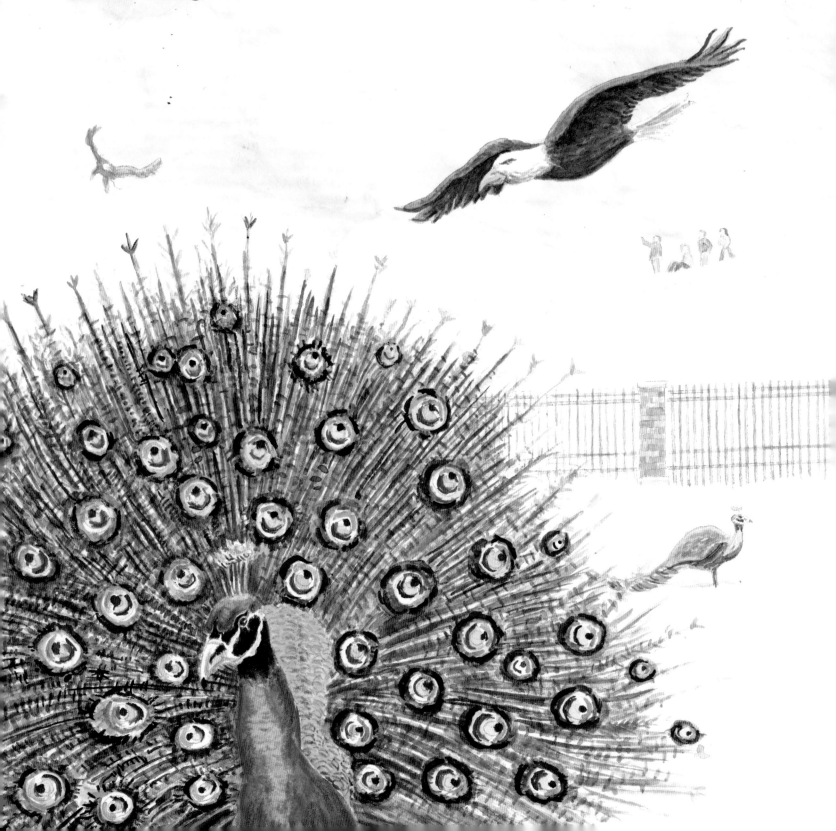

Beasts gathered together to give their Christmas list.

Herman was to make certain, nobody was missed.

The penguins were the first in a very long line.

They never arrived late and were always on time.

They recalled Antarctica's bitter cold and ice.

Snow skis, poles, blue scarves, and warm mittens would be nice.

B. C. Z.
WISH LIST

• Penguins:

• Monkeys:

• Hippos:

Next came the monkeys and chattering chimpanzees,
Tricycles and bicycles were certain to please.

Huge hippos wanted goggles, and bubble bath beads.
An ole' fashion tub would accommodate their needs.

The camels wanted to escape next summer's heat.
Sunglasses, umbrellas and straw hats would be neat.

Slow moving elephants, wrinkly, old, and wise,
Wanted pens, books, and spectacles, what a surprise!

Red tennis shoes and striped socks were the giraffes' dream,
Making them leaders of the best basketball team.

Bears selected honey jars for next winter's nap,
Blue and white pajamas with a red stocking cap.

Lions wanted diamonds, emeralds, and huge feasts.
They were "Lords of the Jungle," and "Kings of the Beasts."

Flamingoes strutted their pink feathers so unique.

Golden earrings and high heels would make them more sheik.

Slow moving turtles were the very last in line.

Surfboards and roller skates certainly would be fine.

Flying reindeer carried Herman's City Zoo list,
To the North Pole through the snow and cold, chilly mist.

Then Santa climbed into his sleigh, packed to the gills.
He knew there would be many surprises and thrills.

While orphan children and beasts slept the night away,
Christmas Eve melted into early Christmas Day.

The zoo animals spotted Santa in the sky,
Dropping ribbon-wrapped presents and waving good-bye.

Each excited beast began to open a gift,
But something was wrong, their confused minds were adrift.

Next to the zoo, the orphans were empty and sad.
They had no Christmas presents, no mother or dad.

Knowing the orphan children had no gifts at all,
Herman gave animals and beasts an urgent call.

Our gifts on this morning, to the children shall go,
Motivation in beasts and animals did grow.

Beasts and animals lined up with great precision,
Truly an amazing Christmas exhibition.

Animals handed their gifts to the next in line.
It was simple, superb, exquisitely divine.

Restless children awoke from their sad winter sleep,
Hoping for Christmas presents piled in a huge heap.

Oodles of gifts for every girl and every boy,
Produced smile-filled faces of happiness and joy.

The children opened their gifts never quite stopping.
The animals rejoiced by flipping and flopping.

One last package from Santa addressed to K. Klaus,
Was carefully opened by Herman with his paws.

A red velvet hat and shiny black boots inside,
A Santa suit labeled "K. Klaus" filled him with pride.

Attached was a short note, stating Herman's new name.
Herman and Kanga Klaus were now one in the same.

With Santa's words Kanga's big heart fluttered and grew.
The Christmas Spirit lives, at the Big City Zoo.